CRAZY DAYS OF

PRINCE

EMEKA PRINCE

Crazy Days of Prince

Table of Contents

GHOST

About to sleep, at 1:10 (yes, in the morning), then wake up, brush my teeth and take a shower, get ready to play soccer (I got a mini tourney tomorrow). In the meantime, I am studying and just doing some quizzes. I will just head to bed now, I am feeling sleepy.

Next day, I noticed something about my life ever since I got into college. Like, I do not know if I am the only one going through this. Generally, I feel so lonely and isolated every time. Almost like I am a ghost (a living ghost hovering around school). It is like people do not see me at all, regardless of my height. I am tall and dark in complexion., so I do not even know how they ignore my presence and do not say a word to me. So, it's super concerning, and I need to get this off my chest here.

Two or three weeks earlier, I had an orientation (a.k.a. Jumpstart), and I did not even meet that many people in my orientation. Nevertheless, I did have a friend of mine that my dad introduced me to. His name is Ife; he is eight out of ten, like has a lot of green flags, which is amazing. He and I are like Day One's because we met each other on the very first day (even the day before school began), before orientation and the opening of the new school year. We know each other well, and we are bros.

The thing is, I am still very isolated and lonely to the point that I am talking to myself a lot (mentally). And every social interaction I have is an awkward one. I did try meeting and interacting with other people, but they keep (instantly) ignoring, avoiding, or dodging me. They cannot even see or smell me; they are always in their mind bubbles. They do not want to look at me (eye-to-eye or face-to-face). They are insecure, traumatized, or just literally ghosting me (ignoring my whole presence). And it just drives me nuts (screws loose), makes me so annoyed and devastated.

I may not look like the BFG (Big Friendly Giant), but I am humanly friendly and funny to hang with (just do not make it awkward). I am friendly as I can be, I just do not comprehend why people do not seem to notice me. No text messages or calls from anybody. I only get attention when I am not in the right mood. People approach me a lot when I am trying to mind my business, not get unnecessary attention, and do my thing.

I do want peace and no problems at all. But I never said I do not want people. I cannot do without people in my life; I need good people to support and hype me up. I am seeking a companion (just one person) that will match my energy and be self-centered toward me (and not other people). A ride and die, stick by brick, skin to skin, back on whack, side by side. Now, I feel like a monster because no one comes to me or greets me (like, hi, hello, how you doing, hafa, how's school, how's life, how u dey, and how are classes?). Maybe it is just the tradition or custom around here, which I am not used to. I like being alone when there is no waste in my sieve.

I have come a long way and a longer way to go, so do I still need someone who will impact my life? It is terrifying, but it is affirmative. The thing is, I truly do not want anything to do with people, but I cannot be a ghost forever. I need to find a way to blend in (not in a crazy way), just in a way that I can adapt and grow. I am trying not to repeat mistakes that I have made in the past. I am patiently waiting for the right people, but I do not even know if they are arriving or have arrived. Like, I do not know if they are there or not there; I just cannot tell. I have made up my mind to come to people, through me (no one else). It is like success; you earn it—it is not given, so you must receive it. Right now, I am so sleepy. I have to go sleep and do things for tomorrow. Good sleep is very important, trust! I will continue tomorrow.

Hey, I am back. Today was not that bad. I just feel like I have messed up in a way (I am not going too deep here). I am gatekeeping with myself. Moving on, I did get noticed a bit today, which is a good thing, to be honest. I was pretty much alone throughout today. I called my mom in the morning (more like a family group call, which I joined.). Today was just there, nothing really went down. I studied my BIO and do some quizzes. Apart from that, today was like my usual days (nothing so crazy). There is nothing in particular I would like to talk about today.

GHOST CONT'D

It has come to my attention that when I am with my friend (like one-on-one), people just approach my friend and start talking to him or her without even realizing that I am there (that I am by their side). They are literally ghosting me at this point. They just cannot see me, just my friend that they see, and I find it so concerning because I am there standing like a tree, and they cannot feel my breeze. It is so frustrating. You get me? Like, I cannot be seen at all, which is crazy, because I am tall and dark. Anyways, I was not looking forward to experiencing this side(atmosphere) of college. Life sucks at the moment, but I have to keep pushing. Sometimes I wish that I could switch bodies for a week and experience real joy. Man! Life (in college) is just tough.

I have never experienced this type of ghosting in my entire life of being a Gen Z. I do have one huge insecurity which affects my social life, which is my face. People have a tendency to judge me a lot based on how I look, but that is not the point I am getting at. I do not want to lock eye contact with people for too long, considering the fact that I have face cramps (my eye twitches out a lot), almost like I got punched by a lotion or some type of irritant. It is not that I am not attractive; it is just that I am very insecure about my face, and people could get frightened when they see me. Right now, I am calculating jump scares per day (no jokes). So, meeting people is a strenuous Israelite journey that I did not pack enough luggage for. Like, a lot to consider physically and mentally. To be sincere, it is so worrisome, and this is my main reason I do not look at people or girls (in particular). I am not trying to be rude or anything,; I just have a very insecure insecurity that disrupts my social life.

I miss my fine -boy, no -pimples era. I looked way more handsome when I was younger (that is just a fact). Teenage era is the worst—so frustrating, depressing, and boring. Kids love their age; teens try to manage the damage at their age (truth about growth). Frankly speaking, childhood is the best hood to be at—not teenhood, not adulthood, not singlehood. When I was a child, I knew little to nothing about life and always assumed teenagers were cool (but they were actually depressed). Childhood be like you can walk around the park butt naked, and people will not care a bit (not a single f's). Also, you can just have all the fun, you want to have; no eyes are on you. Sometimes, I wish I could never grow up and be a child forever.

But it does not work that way (unless I got a time machine). Today I was in class, and we were transitioning into a group discussion, and the people that were next to me completely ghosted me (like I never existed). I really felt so alone (Mr. Lonely). They all switched sides on me, even though I was there, and I was by their sides (literally side to- side), and they faced their own groups and did their activities together.

I also realized this: when I desperately need something, I do not attain it at that moment. But when I am no longer interested in having it, it always comes around (like a temptation I do not want anymore). It drives my mood down. Anyways, life in university is truly depressing for me (at the start). I feel so unimportant, and no one even cares. I just remembered my high school teacher used to say that life in university is so lonely—you are all by yourself and all alone. So, it is like being homeschooled, and you are all by yourself generally.

I gave my journal to a girl to read. She thought of it as a good way to manage my mental health. At first, she thought I was mentally not okay. Then, after a brief discussion with her face to face, she thought of the positivity behind it. At least now she knows it is a therapy book (not a diary). Moving on, I am currently studying my BIOL_O; I got a midterm coming up. It is so stressful, I need a break. Like, wow, I am so packed right now. I still feel ghosted, nevertheless. Right now, I am trying my best not to put my mind on it too much and keep my head up.

Fast Forwarding

I just finished writing my midterm two hours ago. I did not know how I did, plus I was nervous and shaking, but God is with me, and I know He is with me. Right now, I am just getting prepared for the next one (midterm), so I am studying.

Today, I saw this girl in my program (nursing). I tried to approach her by saying hi; she said "hi" back and just completely ignored me, like I was not even there. I tried to get her attention, but she just kept going. I found it rude and disrespectful, so I just left her. Maybe she was not in the mood or somewhat. I do not know why people are like that—just ghosting your fellow brother (left, right, and center). No greetings or salutations, it is very disrespectful, frankly speaking.

I am so tired now. Even though it is midday, I need a nap. But I will relax in a bit (before I nap)—more like no sleep or movement, just calm down, rest my body, and gain some energy. I have an appointment coming up, so I am just waiting. In the meantime, I will be writing (trying to relax). No studying for now; I need a break.

CAME BACK

Nothing much is on my mind right now. I am just in a corner. Not turn back; need to keep moving. Today is a new chapter, a new day. I have decided not to care much about how people behave around me. I will just stick with what I am doing, which is to approach and discuss, meet some new people.

Today I realized that life is just a game (like, literally)—a role-playing game.

Everybody gotta do something that will contribute to the world around them. Everybody gotta have a talent, and desire. Everybody gotta play their own role well (good enough), just for the world to be sustainable. I cannot stay down for long; I can always climb back up..

NO SLEEP

For the past two months I have been in school, I have not been able to have a good or proper sleep (like, home-sweet-home type of sleep). I do not know why. I thought it was because I sleep during the day, but even when I do not sleep during the day, I still cannot sleep properly at night.

I think there are other factors that cause this, like drinking too much water before I go to bed and having the fan faced upon me as I lay down to sleep, which I find very uncomfortable because I usually do not use a fan on me (back home). I often use the air conditioner or heater installed in the house.

So, when the breeze from the fan comes at me, I just feel so cold, and I want to take a piss when I am asleep. So, it is very disruptive to have a fan on me when I am asleep. For this reason, I am going to stop facing the fan on me. I will just leave my windows open for fresh air (ventilation).

Also, I always stay up so late to study, do some work, and enjoy my free time. I might need to change that and start sleeping early so I have good energy when I wake up.

Till now, I still have a hard time closing my eyes. Am I the only one that feels like there is an irritation in my eye that just cramps my face a lot? Even when I sleep and close my eyes, it just hurts so badly. It is exactly like having soap in your eyes when taking a shower—that is what I am talking about. Please, just a caution: never apply lotion on your eyes. You are going to regret it. Trust!!

I MET THIS GIRL

In the evening, I was walking on the hill (staircase), heading down to the dining hall, with my wet hair and dry skin. I saw this girl walking up the hill. She looked at me so romantically. At first, I bitched out (I will admit). But then I changed my mind, and I decided to go back and say something to her, just to test my social skills.

I began talking to her; she felt engaged, so I kept talking. After, I decided to escort her to her dorm because she was heading there. She was like, "That's so sweet." My head blew out like fireworks. So, we were walking and talking on the hill (staircase) and getting to know each other.

As I arrived at her dorm, I just had to ask her this question (just out of curiosity). I do not usually ask this question, but I had to spit it out because she was so fine, like damn. I asked, "Are you single?" and she was like, "Yes." She kinda blushed a bit when I asked that question. She also said, "Yh, I just got outta a relationship." Something recent, I am assuming (in my head).

So, she asked for my contact, so I typed it in for her. She was so fine; I just kept looking at her. See, I am not a face person when it comes to attractiveness, so the fact I am interested in her is something outta my compass (something special). So, when a girl looks so good that her beauty surpasses booty, then yes, I am interested.

Also, in case you were wondering, her name is Sekai. She is also a first year (like me). She is from Hawaii, US. Ethnically, she is Japanese Filipina. I just hope that I am with the right person and my heart does not get broken. I mean, who knows, maybe I am being played. For the moment, I am trying to put my life in one piece, by the goodness and mercies of God. I also need to start associating with people more. If I want to get noticed better, this should be my step one.

the goodness and mercies of God. I also need to start associating with people more. If I want to get noticed better, this should be my step one.

BEEN GONE

Hey, I am back. I have been gone for a while. I have been studying for my midterms (NRSG 115), tryna stay focused and not do too much. Anyways, yesterday I had Thanksgiving. I had to be thankful for a lot of things—the great things that are around and have happened to me (for a reason). Also, I had to be thankful for life itself. It is not easy to be alive today, you know. Not an easy world (more of a cruel and damaged world) I see myself in.

I celebrated my Thanksgiving by calling my family and wishing them a happy Thanksgiving. I went to my friend's house to celebrate with him. Apparently, I came late, so when I arrived, everyone was just chillin' and doin' some work (of theirs). I did have a good stay there. I ate a typical African dish (Nigerian to be exact)—jollof rice and turkey, with some sweet vegetable salad.

I really felt at home and welcomed. Also, I got to hang with my broski, Ife. We have not seen each other lately due to school and responsibilities. I got him a Thanksgiving card to show my appreciation toward him (as a very good friend). I doubt he opened that card or read it at all.

I also got my crush a Thanksgiving card (kinda old school, I know), just to be thankful and admire her. She read it and liked it because it was written by me (a love card specialist). I wrote it in a way that was so empathetic and symbolic.

I genuinely like her, but the truth is, I do not know how she thinks or feels about me. Also, I have faced countless rejections from girls that were totally outta my league. Also, a lot of ghosting, mean words or comments, funny annoying statements, and self- sensitive harsh words (I am gonna stop here, not going too deep.). But you know what I mean.

I just hope that I can pull this off smartly through the grace of God. I have had my eyes on so many other girls, but this one (the special one) just stuck. Moving on, I just hope I am not being brainwashed or mind-played. Mehn, at this moment I am hoping for all the best in my academics, crush situation, and mental aspects of life. God is with me, trust!

In case you wondered how I am doing; I still get ghosted all the time. I just listen to music more and go my way and do my own things. I am so dried up; maybe it is because of the weather. I feel so chilly. Like, laid back in a way, I need sleep.

CONNECTING ALL DOTS

Does my crush really like me, or am I being catfished? Let me start with all the positive signs. She tilts her head every time I talk to her; it is almost like a signal, and she maintains good eye contact whenever I approach her and start a conversation with her.

She looks engaged in my discussion. Also, I am not really a social person who can start good (engaging) conversations like that. I am more of a quiet kind of person, usually by myself, and do not say anything meaningful or interesting.

My crush gives me signals, like at first she introduced me to her friend group, and she told them who I am and what I do. I felt welcomed (my presence was acknowledged, thank God), because most of the time I get sidelined, and I do not feel included at all.

They do not even know I am there, which is crazy because I am Black and also tall. So, I should be very noticeable (people should at least know my face).

My crush also smiles at me when I look at her. It is almost as if she can sense my presence and knows I am there. She gives me heart emojis in text and lovely text messages like, "You're sweet." My crush also asked me for my contact at our first meet-up. I am usually the person who initiates the talking and asks for the other person's contact information, so the fact that she asked me for mine might be a very good sign that she might be feeling me in a way.

These are good signs that she might be into me. But what exactly do I want? What are the personalities that I am looking for in her? Am I really committed to this? Capital no, or am I lookin' for a friend? Let me prioritize this well. This is going to be a slanted response (just a heads up).

I am looking for a lovely -looking person with good intentions, someone who can respect me (mutual respect). Someone I can ride for (roll with) and be myself around—no need to keep an (Oscar - winning) act, just want to be my normal self. I do not mind (I do not care a bit) about race or ethnicity. I just want to feel supported (overall) to do more great things. I am interested in someone who can match my crazy (good humor).

Now, I am a loner, and I did not choose to be one. It more like happened (randomly), and I do not feel good about it. That is why I need to start adopting a new motto: "Do not wait to be approached; go out of your comfort zone to meet new people."

Also, I need to stop overthinking and reading meaning into everything that happens.

As I was saying, Sekai looks good facially and physically, but does she even like me, and what are her intentions? I have not really pinched her enough to get a reaction (a taste of her personality). Also, I need to find something about her that I adore (apart from looking good). For now (I do not know about later), I would say she is empathetic, eloquent, and energetic. I said empathetic 'cause it is almost like she feels my emotions, or I feel hers when we are around each other. She is eloquent 'cause she speaks with a calm voice (not too loud), and she listens well when I speak (not a lot of people do this). Also, I said she is energetic because she has this auratic energy when I am around almost like I feel calm (relaxed) or something. I do not know how to describe it; it is just in the air.

CONNECTING ALL DOTS, PART 2

So, today I am going to dive deeper—more like a search mission. This will involve minor stalking and creep acts. The purpose of this is to get to know her more and observe her personality traits (not just admire her looks). Also, I will have to go into more discussion with her. For some reason, I feel she has a man, and I am being played. When I find her and discuss all this, I will write down my evaluations to know what I am doing and also get more info on her. I need to make sure my assumptions are slightly accurate.

Moving on, today was not that special (or interesting). I did try to meet this girl, but she was a bit insecure and said she had a boyfriend (mind you, I never asked). I asked her if I could walk her to class; she was like, "yeah," then she switched up on me and was like, "sorry, I got a boyfriend." In my head, I was like, damn (that was rude), like who asked? No one (that is right).

I did not even have class today. I thought that I had class (so I was rushing and panicking for no reason) just to get a front row seat, lol! Cause last week there was no free seat in the front rows for me to sit in, so I had to sit alone in the corner of the class (me, my thoughts, and myself). I was given a task (more of an assignment to do). I finished it some hours ago. So, I am chilling and finding something else to do. To be sincere, University is just like having a lesson teacher and staying home all day. It is basically like your lesson teacher giving you assignments or tasks to finish, then grading them later. I barely have any classes or people to talk to (in those classes); it is just me.

Uni is like a small city filled with a bunch of students and multicultural peeps from distinct areas or countries, just trying to fit into the system, make friends, and find purpose. I used a gumball machine to express how university is: "There are green, yellow, red, purple, and blue gumballs, all squeezed into one jar. A kid comes with a coin to get a gumball and chews it till it dries up. Then the kid either digests it or disposes of it." What I am saying is that you come, you go, and get old. You do not always stay fresh and colorful for long (as a gumball). When you work hard and get used, you either get digested or disposed of. In the end, what is left behind is the saliva or dryness placed upon you, just like shit.

People pressure themselves without even enjoying life for once and getting the real feel of it, till they are gone. They call it growing up, maturity, and responsibilities. I call it plain stupidity; it does not make sense at all. For the fact that you try to be validated every time and you want to align with the standards society has of you. It does not seem right for me. As the saying goes, "The world is your oyster"—it is open for you to live in, for free, and to explore.

To be truthful, I do not even think I am the best fit for Sekai. She is so outta my scale—it is almost like a janitor trying to get with his boss, you get me? I need to up my game a little more; apparently, there are levels to this.

SECRET CHAPTER

According to my observations in a social setting, when I avoid eye contact with people, they begin to think I am rude or I am avoiding them. I am obviously not a rude person (more of a goofy, serious -looking mf). I have a deep insecurity about my face, and I do not want people to stare too long at it 'cause they will notice it, then judge me for it. This will just kill my entire self-esteem for that whole day. So, it is a no for me. I can be viewed as rude at times, but the truth is that I am a very insecure person, and I try my best to avoid too much unnecessary attention (people love staring a lot) from people (mostly mean people).

It is difficult, but I just cope by being nonchalant or cracking hilarious jokes for people to laugh at, also praying daily. The thing is, when I am not insecure about my face, people will feel more comfortable around me, and I will not mind approaching anybody. I will feel much more comfortable with myself, but I do not want all this.

I feel like it is much better when I do not show myself often and have to keep a (mature boy) act all the time. I find it classy (like having some class), and people will treat me with more respect because I am quiet and unpredictable. It just shows that I am intelligent; sometimes silence is the best language for fools.

You never need to prove anything when people know little to nothing about you. You just gotta keep the act going. I mean, I can lose myself at times, but I keep it leveled. The best and only way to make people know who you are is by action, and not my mouth (tongue).

YOU MAY WANT, BUT NOT NEED!

Bear with me, I will be shifting topics a bit here. It has come to my realization that I do not really need a relationship at all. I watched a video (Instagram reel) simply talking about how "you may want her, but not need her." You may want somebody to love you; you may want a relationship, but you do not need it—simple as that. This message in the reel just stuck with me. 'Cause at times I always felt like I wanted a girl or I wanted somebody in my life, but realistically I do not need it. It is all a mindset (a terrible one) that I have misunderstood and established upon myself, which is bad.

It is easy to say I want a girl, but not an easy thing to commit to that relationship (say yes). At the end of the day, you do not need it (at all). By the way, Ishowspeed was in this reel, and he said it perfectly, "Ladies is like a weird creature, you know, they don't ever like you, they don't really like you for your own self, you know, they always want something out of you." I totally (100%) agree with what Ishowspeed said because it is just reality, and it sucks.

They all want the fake things. I was with a couple of girls yesterday, just in the lounge, hanging out and gisting. At first, when I joined the room (convo), I came in smooth. I acted as a typical mature person (which I am obviously not). Then after some hours went by, I transitioned into the real version of myself (the creepy, mysterious, unlovable, weird, and special) which I am.

They were all like, "I gotta go," 'cause I was too spooky for them. Yeah, I forgot to add, I was basically creeping them out on purpose when they asked me, "How old am I?" and I replied, "I am not your age," in a suspenseful way. They all guessed various ages (like 18, 19, 20, and even 15), but I was like, "Nah. I'm not an adult or a teenager; I'm way older than you think. I've lived for many years. I live a life; when I die, I reincarnate into a completely different type (or race) of person. So, you wouldn't be able to recognize me.." They all thought I was playin' and joking with them. I looked serious when I said all this.

So, they were falling for it, which was surprising to me. Anyways, that's the gist of it. My point is they all wanted me to leave the room when I switched up on them and acted like this entity that has lived for so many centuries (you get what I mean). I was just being myself (the real me) after having a long-lasting session with the fake version (of myself). That's the whole point. Plus, it was late (like midnight late), so I was lowkey tripping out.

It's so tragic that people do not value the real ones (most especially the dudes). Real dudes do not fake or hide anything. They show themselves regardless of who they are with. Some may behave well, while some may behave badly. But they deserve an applause 'cause it's very hard to find someone that can be themselves and not care what people (around) think of him (them).

Huge respect to Ishowspeed. He's very humble and 100% real with himself and others. I personally think that girls want guys to have a certain standard for themselves, and if a guy can't maintain that standard, he's not fit for purpose, and he is seen as weird.

I'm so flustered because it doesn't make any sense in my opinion. Whenever I see a real person, I feel safe in a way that I know their every move and they don't hide any bad habits (so predictable). It's almost like they embrace it. Shout out to the real ones.

SIDELINING

Today, I hung out with my friend, Brian. I don't know why, but anytime I'm walking with him or by his side, he just gets a lot of attention from other people (celeb effect). It's almost like I am the enzyme and he's the product (in this case). I'm there standing (as usual) while he is having a discussion with his friend(s). And I don't even get noticed or recognized at all. Personally, it's so frustrating, I still don't get why people just tend to come to him a lot when I'm with him and having a good time together.

They don't even say hi or hello to me. Mind you, this has happened to me on numerous occasions (countless numbers of times), and it doesn't seem to stop (any time soon). I like it when my friend is getting all the attention (in the world), but when I'm not getting a single bit of attention from anybody, then that's a problem.

My friend gets all this attention in coincidental meetups and social settings, and I don't even get acknowledged a bit (my presence)—just totally snubbed. And it gets worse; people think they know me, but we don't even talk to each other or have ever met before. So, it just makes everything awkward, and I hate to admit it's annoying. It makes social interaction way more difficult and less engaging—more like you are just by yourself (literally) all the time. You don't get a break from your loneliness.

I'm going to completely switch topics, so stay with me. I noticed something when I'm on the soccer pitch and I'm playing soccer. When I'm talking and shouting (coaching) at my teammates, everyone is silent—no feedback or communication. No one says a word to me. But when I'm quiet and not saying a single word, someone from outta nowhere (just spawns) and starts talking to me like we know each other very well—in a bossy, disrespectful (frowny) manner. And this is minutes (fast-forwarding) after I just finished my shouting (coaching) at my teammates. In my head, I'm like, "This person is talking to me like he's my dad or she's my mom," like, "They don't know me that well to be talking to me like we are besties or have a mutual connection.."

Apparently, we don't converse at all. Next thing, they're giving me speeches, motivational talks, and coaching like we know each other 100% or we are together. It drives me crazy 'cause "this dude thinks he knows me, but he hasn't had a taste or feel of me."

Even outside the soccer pitch, my conversations with people are abstract. It's almost like they want to tell me something, but nothing ever comes out. It's like existing in thought (or as an idea) but not having a physical (solid) existence. In my head, I'm like, "Bro (or girl), just tell me what you are trying to tell me, stop shivering about it, just spit it out." This happens mainly when I'm in public, class, and mostly when I'm on the soccer pitch.

I don't like it at all because it seems as if they want to say something, but nothing ever comes out (Eminem can relate). I've read his lyrics a lot, lol! Picture this—you finish preaching the gospel, and no one converses with you until the end of service.

Maybe someone comes up to you after preaching to tell you something. This is the context of how my conversations with people are.

It is very one-sided and not interesting 'cause I'm either the one doing the talking and they are listening, or they are doing most of the conversation and I'm just there listening. I don't add anything to the conversation. I dislike conversations that are very one-sided and emotionless because they're less engaging and fun.

It has come to my realization that kids relate more with each other than teens or adults ever do. They ask all the good and engaging questions that can put a smile on people's faces. They are funny; they don't brag at all or have all that unnecessary ego. It just makes relationships and friendships sweeter. Sometimes, I just wish I could act more like a kid and be more expressive in my feelings and thoughts. I wish I had a time machine to go back in time and have all the good fun I once experienced.

AT THIS PARTY

Today, I went to this late-night party. It was so not for me. Intimately speaking, I wasn't feeling it at all. I regret wasting my precious money on a ticket I didn't even need. Apparently, I decided to go to a party to see if I could socialize more with people, test my social skills, and not be lonely. I saw this as a major opportunity because this party was for all ages (no limit), and I'm underaged.

So, I can't just go to any party. There must be an age limit in the party that I'm attending (you get me?). The main reason I bought tickets to come to a party (for the first time) was to meet new people and socialize. I'm not a party guy. I find it distracting, and at the end of the day, it's not as fun as I see it in music videos or movies. I got my hopes a bit too high when I bought those tickets online, lol! Right now, my bank balance is crying.

I was so alone at this party, and I wasn't even dancing (moving my body or shaking my hips). I didn't associate with that many people. I was all by myself the whole time, so I decided to meet up with the president of the Student Union Okanagan, Peter.

He was one of the coordinators of the party. I had a very long discussion with him about feeling ghosted and sidelined by people (in conversations, meetings, or events). He is a very open-minded person, listenable, reasonable, and surprisingly very humble. I said surprisingly because I have a lot of experiences with people whereby this person gets a major role, and they just lose their head completely and have the biggest ego on earth.

I respect his humbleness a lot because I really needed it. He's also very helpful and enjoyable to talk with. I was in shock at how humble he is as a person with a high position. He was as humble as an average individual (with no ego attached). Like, he's literally the president of the Students Union Okanagan (SUO), and he was having such an engaging discussion with me (pls, who I be?). Amongst the little to no one I met at that party, he was the most fun to talk to, and it just made me feel hopeful. Give it time—it's just a rough start. It's not going to be easy trying to fit in a social gathering full of teenagers and adults. Being with him made me feel connected and among.

EVERYWHERE PRINCE GOES

Everywhere I go, people are kissing, twirling, twerking, smiling, feeling among, engaging, talking, in a relationship, or even having sex. But I can't even have one simple conversation with someone without being interrupted by a third party. Imma need pop-up blockers (at this point). Like, it's getting outta hand, and I can't even control it.

Two incidents happened to me today while I was at the party. So, I came up to this guy, a cool -looking Black (African) dude. I came to say hi to him and get to know him a bit 'cause this dude looked so much like my cousin, to be sincere. Then, this petite lady came outta nowhere and hugged him (like he won a billion-dollar lottery). I felt so dissed and interrupted 'cause she just popped outta nowhere and started hugging this dude (like they were getting married).

So, I just left them and went somewhere to sit down (just close my eyes and take a break from all this). At that moment, I wished I wasn't even at the party. Another similar event occurred. I decided to meet up with this woman that I met one time (a long time ago). But as soon as I opened my mouth to start a conversation with her, the bartender just interrupted so quickly, like she didn't see me about to open my mouth and talk to this woman. They just started blushing at each other, like they were about to kiss (smooch) each other. They had this long (15-minute convo) and totally left me hanging out there. I was so annoyed (deep down) 'cause at the start of my conversation, she literally halted (interrupted) me and didn't even apologize or add me to their ongoing (long-lasting) conversation.

Sometimes I try my best not to put my mind into things like this, but it just keeps happening (every single day), like non-stop. It's so devastating for me, especially when I'm trying to meet someone and people (third parties) just come outta nowhere and change the whole topic. Like damn, show some respect. I get the fact that your humor is two times the size of planet Jupiter.

I am so not trying to do something stupid or crazy. But as things are now for me, I might just lose myself (I might go outta my mind). That reminds me—today I came so early for the party. In the meantime, I went to the theatre to watch a movie, Sinners. I met this girl in the theatre that I partly knew from track and field. She was able to recognize my face (which I found surprising). We watched Sinners together. I tried to hold her hand 'cause we were sitting closely together (side to side), but she didn't want me to hold her hand.

Lemme fast-forward this. So, at the party, I see her whining her waist toward this guy that I don't even wanna describe ('cause it's so damn killin' me). She was twerking her ass (so ferociously) on his private area (I'm gonna pause). In my head, I was like, hello, we met earlier before the party even started, and in the theatre, I asked to hold your hand during the movie, and you disagreed—but now you are shaking your fine ass on this dude's pickle. Why? Like, why?

So, at that moment, I knew I gotta leave. I couldn't handle watching that unpleasant scene. I had to exit the party. That's the end of the party story. I ain't going to a party like this next time — or a party at all. For sure!

APPOINTMENT DISAPPOINTMENT

So, yesterday I had an eye check -up appointment (more like an eye exam) at 9:00 a.m. in the morning. I set an alarm for 7:45 a.m. (this was right after the party night), so I was so freakin' tired, to be honest. When I finally got to sleep, my eyes felt like they were in a sauna (a very warm one). I slept like a baby boy (for like six hours), then I got up and went to pray, then showered and brushed my teeth.

Dressed up, took the bus to my venue for the appointment, and after I got to my destination, I had to wait an extra 45 minutes outside in the cold weather. Picture this— you're waiting outside with barely any coverage on your body, and wind is just stabbing your soul (right, left, right, and centre). You couldn't find a store to shelter yourself 'cause they were all closed (at that time). That was my situation. And when the eye (optometry) doors finally opened, a family of three came outta nowhere and went in before me. I was kind to them because they were together (as a family)—a man, his wife, and their daughter (who probably had an appointment).

Just to show my maturity, I let them proceed before me, even though I had just waited in the freezing cold for an hour. When I came in, this man (the receptionist) was like, "What's my name?" I told him my name, Emeka Prince, and he was like, "Am I Emeka?" I said, "Yes." Then he asked, "Where's my health card?" I gave it to him, and he said, "This card can't be used. I need your MSP card." Apparently, it was my SaskHealth card that I gave him, and in my head, I thought I could use my SaskHealth card in any province (without any obstacles or problems) 'cause I'm a PR. But unfortunately, I couldn't use it.

So, he asked, "Do you have your MSP (Medical Service Plan) card?" I replied, "No, I applied for it. My card is coming in the next two months." Of course, I didn't have it with me. So, after six minutes of frustration, I tried to negotiate this out. I tried convincing him that I don't have my MSP. All I have is my SaskHealth card. He even expected me to pay $70 bucks outta my pocket just for a flippin' ten-minute eye exam (check -up).

In my head, I tried to knock this man out—my face said it all (the rage was there). Like, what the hell? I woke up so early this morning for this (trash -ass) ten-minute eye check-up appointment that was even rescheduled (I missed my earlier appointment). Mind you, I didn't have a single dime in my account at all, or even close to $70 bucks. So, I just left the shit eye (optometry) store or place (I don't even know what they call it). I headed out with no words, no further negotiations, and a lot was going through my mind (many things).

This man (receptionist) just wanted money from me (whatta fraudster) for a flippin' ten-minute (shit-ass) eye check-up.

Please, who's gonna pay $70.0 bucks just for a 10-min eye check-up?

Not me. I'm too street smart for this baby scam (too cheap—try harder next time!). I had to find a medical center that was open at the time, and I came across "Urgent and Primary Care Centre," which was in my location. So, I had to find the nearest bus stop, waited for a bus, then took the bus from where I was to the UPCC. I was so damn pissed, but I stayed faithful, hoping that I wouldn't have to pay a dime (just to check up my eye) and could get some help (see a specialist).

Forgot to mention, throughout last week my right eye was twitching a lot. I had terrible eye fatigue in my right eye, partly in my left eye too, and it made me so uncomfortable—especially when

I'm talking with a fine chick or people —because I felt that something (external) was stabbing my right eye, and I didn't want anyone to notice it at all. If not, they might start mimicking me or judging me. My right eye was just killin' me for like a week.

Anyways, where did I stop? I had an eyeache in my right eye and partly in my left. I had to meet with a nurse at the UPCC; she then referred me to a social worker and a physician. These two people really helped me, and it was worth the wait (I waited for about three hours in the waiting room) just to meet these amazing people. The social worker was very listenable and understanding toward my feelings and words. It was very engaging speaking with her, and it helped me wonderfully. I'm not going to disclose what I discussed with the social worker (for confidentiality reasons).

To be sincere, it was worth my time, and I really appreciated her approach toward me. I felt very welcome, and she didn't back out (not a lot of people do this). She supported me mentally and gave me hope. It was very supportive talking with someone, and the person listens and doesn't judge (during the whole conversation).

The physician also helped me a lot. He checked up my eye and didn't find any problems with it. I was astonished 'cause I thought I had a problem with my eye—maybe the problem just disappeared (all of a sudden). I benefited a lot talking with him. He was extremely nice and friendly toward me, and he understood every word that came out of my mouth (people don't usually get me). He gave smart responses and simple words of wisdom, which I tend to forget all the time. I found this helpful to me, and may God bless him, and her (the social worker). They really made my day.

I WISH…

Sometimes, I just pray that people were more listenable and less judgmental toward other people who are going through so many things. It would be so beneficial to the society we find ourselves in. Think about it—no gossip, no side talk, and no fake personalities. The world would be so different in a good way (more like a utopia), and people would understand each other better without being someone else, but themselves.

LATE FOR CHURCH

I decided to enjoy my sleep today because I didn't get enough sleep last night, so today was my night (to refresh). I woke up around 10:00 a.m., not sure the specific time, but it was just around 10:00 a.m. My spirit was just telling me to wake up and go to church (I didn't even feel like it, 'cause I was sleepy), and I was even going to be late. I contemplated just doing an online service rather than going to church.

Regardless of how sleepy I was, I got up and got ready to spend my day with God in church. After service, I connected with a retired pastor, Mr. Nick, and he prayed for me and my family's well-being. He was just so amazing, and he connected me with fantastic Nigerian people (these are very good people), and I felt among (part of their conversation). I swapped numbers and gestures (handshakes and greetings) with these people, and they were just so delightful to talk with. They are totally amazing people.

Mr. Nick even offered to get me something from the café in the church. It was so nice of him—like eye-opening for me—because people usually dodge or avoid me. This man was so outgoing, and he even offered to give me a ride back to campus, and I didn't have to take the smelly bus (people piss in the buses).

Like, we had meaningful discussions with each other after the church service, and it amazed me a lot because I usually get the feeling that I'm an outcast everywhere I go, and people don't approach me at all or even talk to me without dropping an item on the floor or flinching (for no reason). I must be an alien (not human-like) for people to act that way toward me.

I find it very disturbing for them because they judge from their skin and face and do not actively get to meet or interact with the person. So, they think they know me, but they actually don't know a dime about me. I get brain-bumps when someone spawns outta nowhere, approaches me, and treats me like I'm a person—like I'm one of them. I find it surprising because I don't usually get approached at all or talk to people as much. The reason is, I get judged a lot by people, just telling from their facial expressions, body language, and reactions.

I'm not trying to get roasted (verbally abused), so anytime I meet someone, I just hope they are okay and not feeling insecure or uncomfortable (things like that). I want it to be mutual and not one-sided. So, when I'm with a girl (in particular), I would try to be more friendly, talk in a friendly and funny manner. But when I'm with a guy, I'm the total opposite. I'm not as engageable, outgoing, or as friendly as I am when I'm conversating with a girl. It's just complex (don't worry too much about it). I like to be myself regardless of who's around, but the people that come by (are around) are always filled with negativity (no positive energy at all)..

TODAY WAS STH...

I had a Term 2 information session this morning, but I couldn't make it 'cause I had to sleep in (so tired of these early morning activities). It was a very important session, which I missed. I had an online class which I attended late 'cause I was trying to locate the coordinator for my nursing practice placement course. I was trying to find her 'cause she was in charge of the site selector for my practice placement course. (I'm not going too deep on this).

So today I got my package from Temu. It got this silver ring and a silvery rosary necklace (for fashion). It got a cross on it. I will wear it every single day to take God with me everywhere I go. Now I know I'm safe and untouchable.

This chapter has come to an end. I wish I could say more, but I have run outta words. See ya, in the next series.

CONTRACT RELATIONSHIP

I have been thinking of a way to get a girl without true intimacy or love match (tick her checklist). So, I came up with an idea in which I can date a girl for a specific amount of time (days or months). The idea is contract relationship, you get a 1-week free trial (firstly, when you sign, no payment) Lol! After that we start talking (talking stage and getting to know eachother). Thirdly, we get to invest in eachother (put our money on ourselves). Fourthly, we start dating (kissing, hugging, touching, hanging out, and all that). This should finalize (solidify) the relationship, and the best part about this type-a relationship, is that you get to create your own contract, you can add all the terms and conditions, agreements, red flags and green flags, turn off's and turn on (all that stuff). Also, (not to forget) you should add your name and desired partner's name, input your signatures, to seal up the deal. Some addons to this contract relationship is that, after the 1-week free trial, you can choose to continue or discontinue (depending on your interest), and choose an extension like, 1-month, 5-months, or 1-year. The extensions vary, (depending on how long you want to continue). After such extension, you can always renew or no renew (depending on how you feel about each other). The rules are regulated in yourselves, there's no head or body in this type-a relationship. Overall, I think this is a good vision(idea) for people who want to start an ideal relationship with someone or go deeper from (just friends) type-a relationships.

HUGE MESS

Today, I had this soccer game (intramural tourney). The winner gets free T-shirts; my team made it to the play-offs. So, we made it through the semi's and we moved into the finals. Lemme talk about how the semi's went, I played well (just okay, not the best). We conceded four goals, and scored five goals (thanks to our goal machine). I was too anxious to keep playing (the intensity was too high for me). So I dipped second-half (partly). I did play a huge part in the game. But, they (opponents) almost came back, they had a star player (don't know his name). But, he was a playmaker in their team (and lowkey carried his team). The other team also got fans with posters (and all that). But, my team had ourselves (and that's all we needed).

Moving on, we (my team) squeezed through the semi's and entered the finals.

Things went down (like intense crazy things), the score was levelled. Till I flopped at the back, and they (other team) used it to their advantage, and we conceded a goal (unlucky). The game went on (second half). We scored again in the second half (making it tied). The game kept goin' then my teammate attempted clearing the ball, to keep the ball away from our box (so they don't score) then it deflected on my teammate, and we conceded another goal.

The game was 3-2 (for us), we kept fighting back, I got the ball, ran with it to the box, and fell. I was given a penalty, at first, I didn't want to take it cause' I have 0 aim, and 99 shot power. One of my teammates wanted to take it. But I insisted to take it, so I stepped up to take the penalty, I didn't place it, and I missed. This was going to tie the game. I felt so shit, terrible, I should just quit (at this point).

I just ruined my day and everybody's day. And even when things were bad, it still got worse cause' I was given a pass (thru ball) by my teammate, and this dude from nowhere, just clashed up on me, and damaged my thigh (my thigh felt so broken). It was almost swollen, I began limping, so I had to exit the pitch. I was on the sidelining growling in pain, and the dude that did this to me (didn't even say sorry or apologize). If I had two good legs at that time (I could have gone for payback and beat the hell outta that dude, regardless of who was watching).

But my left thigh was destroyed, so I couldn't do shit. I could only watch my team keep fighting (and giving their all) from the sidelines. Then, after I felt a bit of relief from my damaged left thigh, I requested a sub-in, to keep playing for my team. But, due to time (there were only seconds left), and the game was about to end, (what do I mean about to end?), the other time were literally wasting time, so the game ended (after some seconds).

I felt disappointed with myself, and to my team. We came this far and we lost. I took three L's in one match, actually four (whatta terribly bad evening). A broken left thigh, a missed crucial penalty, lost the game, and I didn't get acknowledgement from anybody, or from the dude that destroyed my left thigh (like, God sakes).

After the match I was so down (demotivated), like I always come to practice by myself every day(rainy days, cold days, hot days, and bad days, in general), and I couldn't even sink in a penalty. What the hell is wrong with me? I felt like crying, I just wanted to be alone, by myself (and not get any unnecessary attention) or bragger next to me. I had to walk from the pitch to my campus (residence) limping with a broken left thigh (do you know how painful that is?), like it was so enduring for me. I was tired, head down, not happy at all, disappointed with myself, and my leg was ruined for the evening. I felt like killin' myself, after all the negative things that had happened.

I felt like the unluckiest person on planet earth, no aura, no people, no self- motivation, and no interest (fun) within myself. Just pure depressing dryness, loneliness is a sickness (please, I need a cure).

I don't even want to interact with people as much cause' they are always bragging, and they don't even acknowledge other people's (like myself) presence. It is a sad reality that I don't like inflicting on myself (at all). But it is always there, so now I gotta talk about it. Damn, people can be very insensitive to other people around them, and all they care about is themselves (their joy and self-accomplishment).

The other day, I was with my crush (hanging out with two of her friends), I wouldn't say hanging, more like being a tree. They were talking about stuff, like my cat, and something else (so specific). I couldn't even join the convo cause' they were talking about things that I can't relate to, also things that were just way to specific, like going to travel to Vancouver for reading week, hanging out with friends and more friends, and petting my cat (I love me cat). Like, switch the convo, so I can participate in, I got no cat or pets (you forgot I'm black?).

All I did while they were talking amongst themselves was listening to my sweet music (I did lower my volume) to listen to what they are talking about, and it wasn't interesting at all. The only reason for even coming to their surrounding (or meet area). Was to talk to my crush, and get to know what's up? With her, apparently, she blocked me all of a sudden, so I have been searching around (looking) for her, to get to know why she blocked me. And after 1hr30mins of being a human tree. We got outside and finally talked. I got the reason to why she blocked me, and why she don't communicate with me at all.

I don't know if I should disclose this, but I gotta do what I gotta do. So, this chick (girl) is bisexual, and she already had a girlfriend (at the moment), "something recent," she said. I felt so down and disappointed of course. I thought I was in the moment of getting with her. But she was just playin' with my feelings, it is a good thing we didn't get too intimate (with eachother). If not, I will feel way worsened (mentally). Once, she admitted about it, I had to back out for two reasons; she is already in an intimate (girl-to- girl) relationship and I don't want to step in the way (stuff like that), also I'm not a fan of LGBTQ (no serious offence), like I don't support gayism, homosexuality, and all that. I just don't (for some reason), like it's a turn off for me. Like, it's that bad. I respect it, but I don't partake in it or actively support it.

BROKEN HEART

This is just a continuation of what was written in the previous chapter (series). As I said earlier, I don't support LGBTQ, I have a strict custom, in which I have to adhere to. And regardless of the custom, I still don't want to support LGBTQ. It's really that personal.

I've always thought, why be gay? when God created two distinct separate genders. The sayin' goes "be fruitful and multiply," I just don't understand why there are several unique boys in this world (and you decide to be fruitful with the same gender). It don't match up, let it be levelled (1 for each).

I was so surprised when my crush admitted, "I'm bi, I have a girlfriend" like it didn't make sense to my hearing. I had to ask again, you say what? cause' I thought she had a man (a boyfriend), this tall Asian dude that I see her hanging around with (all the time), so in my senses (this didn't make ¼ sense to me). I was disappointed (as hell) cause' she looked so perfect (outwardly). I even thought this was the girl God sent from above.

Apparently, my calculations were so wrong. I just overthinked the whole crush situation. And assumed things that I wasn't meant to assume. But it's part of the process, to find the true one. I must end the whole crush situation here, cause' now there's no hope (she's already taken by a girl), you know. I gotta find someone else (within my league). I have to start on a fresh sheet of paper and take corrective action.

SPOKE SOON

Just when I assumed things were goin' well for me, I threw it all in the garbage. I booked a therapy session online. I decided to meet with someone that I could talk to (in private). The pain was still there; I was enduring it all. So, after a week. I met up with this therapist, Amanda (my usual go to). I spoke about all the good things, that were going well for me. One of the good things, I spoke about was, I got invited to join this club, ASCS (a club on Campus). I was yapping about how I got an upcoming meeting with the club, and all the good shit.

That was when I realized, I had made a huge mistake (I spoke too soon). I'm gonna fast-forward, the senior admins of the clubc, scheduled a meeting with me, in the bookstore building. At first, I thought the meeting was for sharing money, hype, or further details I needed to know, while being invited to the club. But it was the total opposite, I was unexpectedly being kicked out of the club, for reasons (I don't want to even talk about). I was being kicked out in a meeting session type-a way (classy).

I'm just going to admit the reasons (I think) why I was kicked out of the club. So, there have been discussions goin' around about me, like he's a creep (anti-social) type-a discussions, that I was unaware of. People say terrible things about me (and not address the good things), so I'm just assuming (not sure) that the senior admins of the club got some awareness (attention) about it. And they are trying to uphold their reputation as a club and not let a moody (pessimistic) teen like me, wreck it up. Apparently, the club is ten years old and is a big (social) club in Campus, they host exotic, entertaining, and social gathering activities.

So, the senior admins or people around observed my behavior (anti-social), and lame energy, I was exhibiting. So, they decided to ex me out. These are my assumptions to why I got kicked out of a club. And the query thing, is that I was the only one that was kicked out of the club. It's so painful, I try to not let it bring my emotion down. Like, I'm just trying to feel engaged in society, and people don't want me round, Wow! It's realistically heartbreaking. And I don't feel it is a good thing to do to someone (like myself), who's trying to fit in, engage, and be part of something.

I played it cool (like I didn't care) when they broke the news to me, at the meeting. I wasn't expecting that at all, like I said earlier, I was expecting money sharing, hype, and promotion (or sth). But not being kicked outta a club. I'm so devastated (shattered). But I will find a way to feel engaged and be part of society. Someway or the other.

FREE PRINTER

This is unbelievable, but I got a completely free printer (that works perfectly well). I got this printer on Facebook marketplace. I couldn't believe it was free, (it is such a useful device, at least add some tag to it). Believe this or not, in UBCO, you need to pay to print pages, docs (all that). So, getting a free printer that I can use at ease. Is very much handy (convenient).

I had to wake up so early, to take a morning bus to the seller's address. It was an hour and some minutes long. This is the longest bus ride I've ever been on, in my current location. It was so long, and after that, I still had to walk about twenty-eight to thirty minutes to the seller's house. And when I finally arrived, the seller wasn't home. I rang her doorbell (like 300 times), and no one answered. So, I contacted her, online (on Facebook) to let her know I've arrived to pick up my printer. I waited for a response, she took so long to reply, and I was outside in the freezing cold (at least I got good covering, this time). There was a basketball court (more like a park) outside, so I was just camping there, in the meantime. While, I wait for her arrival (she wasn't home). She told me she will only be available at 12:20-12:25pm, It was 10:20pm, she texted me this. I had to wait an additional 1hr for a huge ass (black) printer. When she finally arrived, I got my printer.

It was so dusty and musty, and huge. It couldn't fit in my tiny-ass backpack. It is a good thing I came prepared, cause' in the morning, when I was about to depart for this printer Israelite journey. My spirit told me, "get a bag, to carry the printer" my spirit guided me well, apparently there was no bag the printer came with, and I'm not tryna carry a huge dusty-ass printer on my big head. So, I got this large-size Dollarama bag, that fitted perfectly for the huge printer. It saved me stress, and embarrassment. I'm not tryna get unnecessary attention for carrying a big printer, down the hilly road, all the way to the bus stop (28-minute walk, don't forget). So, the bag saved me, and my spirit included.

I took this printer from the seller's house to my house (residence). And cleaned it up (squeaky & tidy, clean) and set it up. It works perfectly well. I just figured how to get it working (start this baby up). For it to work, it has to be in sync, like have the exact same network with your device (laptop or phone), click on the document, you want to print, and select the amount of pages, and color (if you want color), then select or add the printer to your device, and ensure the wifi network is the same with that of the printer.

Then click print, then it prints out all your documents, pages, and all that. Simple, Efficient, and Cost effective (free). Whatta investment, Now I don't need to pay to print, I can save up bucks and print as much as I want. Without having to think of how many lecture notes is going to eat up my precious money. Cause' there are times I had to pay within 50-200 bucks just to print my stuff (no jokes). I've spent a lot on printing, which is something I could've easily avoided from day one.

PEACE OUT, SEE YA...

Forgot to introduce myself formally, allow me to reintroduce myself, my name is Emekus Ndiba Aham, If you are wondered what my name means, it doesn't have an exact meaning or message that comes with it (Not something you can google, and get a serious answer).

So, let me explain the meaning, Emekus, is what I call myself when I feel low, demotivated, and rock bottom (shed). I use it to build my self-esteem, go crazy, feel bold, do crazy things, and catch cruise (as they say). It helps me get loose; it's like an alien-like creature attached to my inner self (like, an alter ego). I use it to go crazy and feel more confident. Ndiba, is my other name (attached to Emekus), it actually has a meaning (surprisingly), it means, "the one who guides' or 'the one who knows' it has wisdom attached to it and is easy to write and pronounce. It is one of my other alter ego's I use to cure worldliness (material things), and stay faithful, keep my head up, and keep goin'. In this state, everything is in the mind and spiritual (so nothing, physically bothers me), while in this state I can't care less. And I feel so free, and happy, I crack stupid jokes for people to laugh and get along. Some people can take it personally. But, as I said earlier, I can't care less (even if they insult me or punch me). Still Emekus Ndiba, I just can't let it bother me. The name, Aham, means, "my name" in my native language. This isn't an alter ego, or anything like that. I just thought it is cool when you say it together, "Emekus Ndiba Aham" it is just luscious, when you say it together (in unison). It adds some taste to the entire name (alter egos).

Moving on, I have a billion things (reoccurring crazy, unexpected, & unusual events) I would like to display in this text, but I have to sit back and relax, to see what's next. I wish I can keep yapping about how crazy my days were. I will keep writing, talking, and addressing crucial messages like these, I will make it broader, and much more entertaining. For now, I'm just observing from a distance what would happen next. I must say goodbye, see ya…….

48

THE END

www.ingramcontent.com/pod-product-compliance
Lightning Source LLC
Chambersburg PA
CBHW040843010826
48978CB00012BB/884

6. Cashew Cream Sauce

INGREDIENTS

- 1 cup soaked cashews
- 1/2 cup water
- 2 tablespoons nutritional yeast
- 1 garlic clove
- Juice of 1/2 lemon
- Salt and pepper to taste

INSTRUCTIONS

1. Blend soaked cashews, water, nutritional yeast, garlic, and lemon juice until smooth.

2. To taste, add salt and pepper for seasoning.

3. Use as a creamy sauce for pasta, veggies, or as a dip.

NUTRITION INFO:

Fat: 60%, Protein: 10%, Carbs: 30%, Total Calories: ~70

7. Almond Milk Hot Chocolate

INGREDIENTS

- 1 cup unsweetened almond milk
- 2 tablespoons cocoa powder
- 1-2 tablespoons honey or sweetener of choice
- 1/2 teaspoon vanilla extract
- Pinch of cinnamon (optional)

INSTRUCTIONS

1. In a saucepan, heat almond milk over medium heat.

2. Whisk in cocoa powder, sweetener, vanilla extract, and cinnamon until well combined.

3. Heat until desired temperature, stirring occasionally.

4. Serve hot.

NUTRITION INFO:

Fat: 50%, Protein: 10%, Carbs: 40%, Total Calories: ~80

8. Rice Milk Pudding

INGREDIENTS

- 2 cups rice milk
- 1/2 cup arborio rice
- 2 tablespoons maple syrup
- 1 teaspoon vanilla extract
- Ground cinnamon for garnish

INSTRUCTIONS

1. In a pot, combine rice milk, arborio rice, maple syrup, and vanilla extract.

2. Simmer on low heat, stirring frequently until the rice is tender and the mixture thickens (about 30-40 minutes).

3. Take it off the burner, let it cool, then store it in the fridge.

4. Sprinkle it with ground cinnamon before serving.

NUTRITION INFO:

Fat: 20%, Protein: 5%, Carbs: 75%, Total Calories: ~120

9. Hemp Milk Smoothie

INGREDIENTS

- 1 cup hemp milk
- 1 ripe banana
- Handful of spinach
- 1 tablespoon almond butter
- Optional: 1 tablespoon chia seeds

INSTRUCTIONS

1. Blend hemp milk, banana, spinach, almond butter, and chia seeds until smooth.
2. Serve immediately.

NUTRITION INFO:

Fat: 40%, Protein: 15%, Carbs: 45%, Total Calories: ~150

Fish and fish products
1. Grilled Salmon

INGREDIENTS

- 4 salmon filets
- Olive oil
- Lemon juice
- Salt and pepper

INSTRUCTIONS

1. Turn the heat up to medium-high on the grill.

2. Brush salmon filets with olive oil and lemon juice. Season with salt and pepper.

3. Grill for about 4-5 minutes per side until cooked through.

NUTRITION INFO:

Fat: 50%, Protein: 50%, Carbs: 0%, Total Calories: Varies based on serving size

2. Baked Cod with Herbs

INGREDIENTS

- 4 cod filets
- 2 tablespoons olive oil
- 1 tablespoon of freshly chopped herbs (parsley, rosemary, or thyme)
- Salt and pepper
- Lemon wedges for serving

INSTRUCTIONS

1. Turn the oven on to 375°F, or 190°C.

2. Place cod filets on a baking sheet lined with parchment paper. Drizzle with olive oil.

3. Sprinkle with fresh herbs, salt, and pepper.

4. Bake for 15-20 minutes until the fish flakes easily with a fork.

5. Serve with lemon wedges.

NUTRITION INFO:

Fat: 35%, Protein: 65%, Carbs: 0%, Total Calories: Varies based on serving size

3. Tuna Salad

INGREDIENTS

- 2 cans tuna, drained
- 1/4 cup Greek yogurt
- 2 tablespoons diced red onion
- 2 tablespoons diced celery
- 1 tablespoon lemon juice
- Salt and pepper to taste
- lettuce leaves or whole-grain bread for dipping.

INSTRUCTIONS

1. In a bowl, mix tuna, Greek yogurt, red onion, celery, lemon juice, salt, and pepper.
2. Serve on lettuce leaves or as a sandwich filling.

NUTRITION INFO:

Fat: 20%, Protein: 80%, Carbs: 0%, Total Calories: Varies based on serving size

4. Lemon Garlic Shrimp Skewers

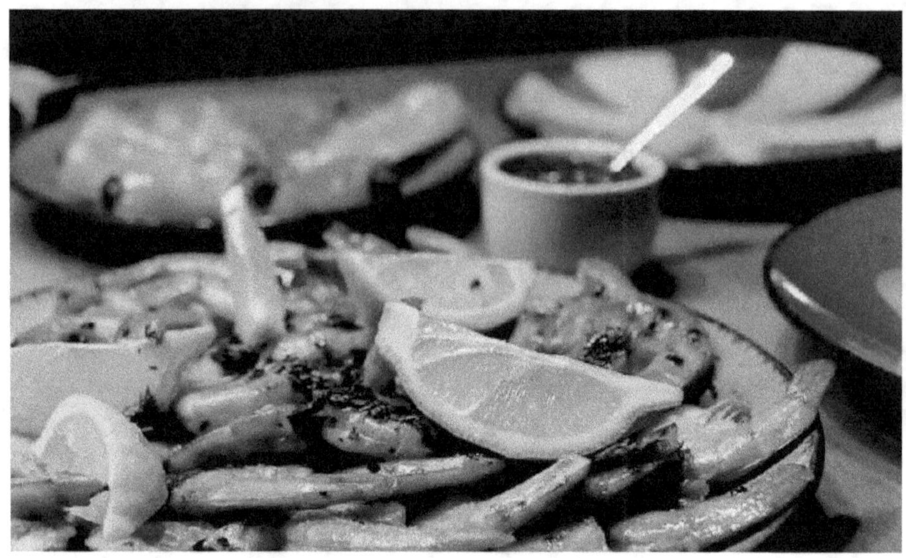

INGREDIENTS

- 1 pound large shrimp, peeled and deveined
- 2 cloves garlic, minced
- Zest and juice of 1 lemon
- 2 tablespoons olive oil
- Salt and pepper

INSTRUCTIONS

1. In a bowl, mix garlic, lemon zest, lemon juice, olive oil, salt, and pepper.

2. Thread shrimp on skewers and brush with the lemon garlic mixture.

3. Grill for 2-3 minutes per side until shrimp turn pink.

NUTRITION INFO:

Fat: 40%, Protein: 60%, Carbs: 0%, Total Calories: Varies based on serving size

5. Pan-Seared Halibut

INGREDIENTS

- 4 halibut filets
- 2 tablespoons butter or olive oil
- 2 cloves garlic, minced
- 1 tablespoon chopped fresh parsley
- Salt and pepper

INSTRUCTIONS

1. Season halibut filets with salt and pepper.

2. In a skillet, heat butter or olive oil over medium-high heat.

3. Add minced garlic and cook for 1 minute. Add halibut filets and cook for 4-5 minutes per side until golden and cooked through.

4. Garnish with fresh parsley before serving.

NUTRITION INFO:

Fat: 40%, Protein: 60%, Carbs: 0%, Total Calories: Varies based on serving size

6. Grilled Swordfish Steaks

INGREDIENTS

- 4 swordfish steaks
- 2 tablespoons olive oil
- Juice of 1 lemon
- 1 teaspoon dried oregano
- Salt and pepper

INSTRUCTIONS

1. Set the grill's temperature to medium-high.

2. Brush swordfish steaks with olive oil and lemon juice. Season with dried oregano, salt, and pepper.

3. Grill for about 4-5 minutes per side until cooked through.

NUTRITION INFO:

Fat: 45%, Protein: 55%, Carbs: 0%, Total Calories: Varies based on serving size

7. Smoked Salmon Salad

INGREDIENTS

- 1 cup smoked salmon, flaked
- Mixed salad greens
- 1/4 red onion, thinly sliced
- 1 tablespoon capers
- 1 tablespoon olive oil
- Lemon wedges for serving

INSTRUCTIONS

1. On a plate, arrange mixed salad greens.

2. Top with flaked smoked salmon, red onion slices, and capers.

3. Drizzle with olive oil and serve with lemon wedges.

NUTRITION INFO:

Fat: 40%, Protein: 60%, Carbs: 0%, Total Calories: Varies based on serving size

8. Grilled Tuna Steaks with Sesame

INGREDIENTS

- 4 tuna steaks
- 1/4 cup soy sauce or tamari
- 2 tablespoons sesame oil
- 2 tablespoons sesame seeds
- Salt and pepper

INSTRUCTIONS

1. In a shallow dish, mix soy sauce or tamari, sesame oil, and sesame seeds.

2. Season tuna steaks with salt and pepper, then coat with the sesame mixture.

3. Grill for 2-3 minutes per side until desired doneness.

NUTRITION INFO:

Fat: 45%, Protein: 55%, Carbs: 0%, Total Calories: Varies based on serving size

9. Fish Tacos with Tilapia

INGREDIENTS

- 4 tilapia filets
- 2 tablespoons olive oil
- 1 teaspoon chili powder
- 1/2 teaspoon cumin
- 1/2 teaspoon paprika
- Corn or flour tortillas
- Coleslaw mix or shredded cabbage
- Sliced avocado, salsa, lime wedges for serving

INSTRUCTIONS

1. Mix olive oil, chili powder, cumin, and paprika. Coat tilapia filets with the spice mixture.

2. Heat a skillet over medium heat and cook the tilapia for 3-4 minutes per side until cooked through.

3. Heat tortillas and assemble tacos with coleslaw mix, cooked tilapia, sliced avocado, salsa, and a squeeze of lime.

NUTRITION INFO:

Fat: 35%, Protein: 50%, Carbs: 15%, Total Calories: Varies based on serving size

Conclusion

As we reach the culmination of this culinary expedition through the realms of low glycemic load cooking, we bid adieu, yet our journey towards flavorful wellness continues. 'Flavors of Wellness' isn't just a book—it's a manifesto, an ode to the marriage of taste and health that resonates beyond these pages.

In our quest for culinary innovation, we've discovered that health need not be sacrificed at the altar of taste. 'Flavors of Wellness' serves as a beacon, guiding us to savor every meal, cherishing the symphony of flavors while nurturing our bodies.

Through chapters dedicated to unraveling the mysteries of glycemic load, we've empowered ourselves with knowledge, fostering a deeper understanding of how food impacts our well-being. Armed with this wisdom, we've embarked on a journey to reshape our relationship with food—where every bite becomes a conscious step towards a healthier lifestyle. The recipes within these pages aren't just a list of instructions; they're an invitation to explore the artistry of cooking, a canvas upon which to express creativity while prioritizing nutrition. From indulgent breakfasts to savory dinners, each dish carries the essence of a mindful approach to eating— where taste isn't compromised but enhanced by wholesome ingredients.

We've ventured into the heart of culinary craftsmanship, discovering the magic of ingredients and the alchemy of their combinations. 'Flavors of Wellness' doesn't limit; it liberates our culinary imaginations, encouraging experimentation and adaptation to suit personal tastes and preferences.

As we conclude this chapter, let's carry forward the spirit of 'Flavors of Wellness.' Let's celebrate the joy of nourishing our bodies while indulging in delightful flavors. Let this cookbook be a constant companion, guiding us towards healthful living without sacrificing the pleasure of a delicious meal. May every meal we prepare, every bite we savor, be a testament to the beautiful amalgamation of taste and wellness. 'Flavors of Wellness' isn't just a cookbook; it's a philosophy—a testament to the belief that healthful eating isn't a chore but a delightful journey—one that we embark upon every time we step into the kitchen.

Farewell, dear reader, but remember—our journey towards flavorful wellness is a continuum, and 'Flavors of Wellness' is our trusted guide. Let's continue savoring the flavors of health, one delectable recipe at a time!

Glycemic load
Diet planner

Dates
____

	BREAKFAST	LUNCH	DINNER	SNACKS
MON				
TUE				
WED				
THU				
FRI				
SAT				
SUN				

Shopping list

Note

Glycemic load

Diet planner

Dates 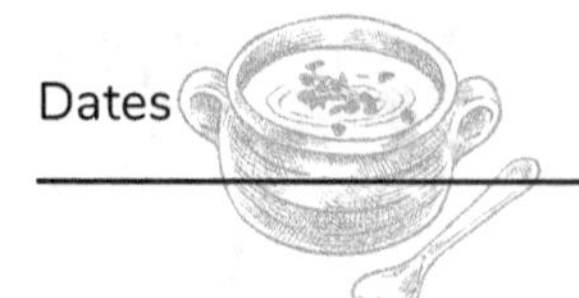

	BREAKFAST	LUNCH	DINNER	SNACKS
MON				
TUE				
WED				
THU				
FRI				
SAT				
SUN				

Shopping list

Note

Glycemic load

Diet planner

Dates

	BREAKFAST	LUNCH	DINNER	SNACKS
MON				
TUE				
WED				
THU				
FRI				
SAT				
SUN				

Shopping list

Note

Glycemic load
Diet planner

Dates
____

	BREAKFAST	LUNCH	DINNER	SNACKS
MON				
TUE				
WED				
THU				
FRI				
SAT				
SUN				

Shopping list

Note

Glycemic load
Diet planner

Dates ___________________

	BREAKFAST	LUNCH	DINNER	SNACKS
MON				
TUE				
WED				
THU				
FRI				
SAT				
SUN				

Shopping list

____

Note

Glycemic load
Diet planner

Dates

	BREAKFAST	LUNCH	DINNER	SNACKS
MON				
TUE				
WED				
THU				
FRI				
SAT				
SUN				

Shopping list

Note

Glycemic load

Diet planner

Dates

	BREAKFAST	LUNCH	DINNER	SNACKS
MON				
TUE				
WED				
THU				
FRI				
SAT				
SUN				

Shopping list

Note

# Glycemic load
Diet planner

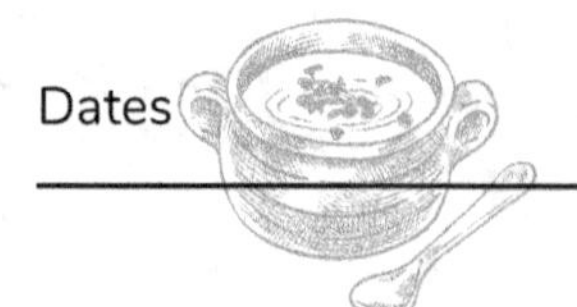
Dates

	BREAKFAST	LUNCH	DINNER	SNACKS
MON				
TUE				
WED				
THU				
FRI				
SAT				
SUN				

Shopping list

Note

Glycemic load

Diet planner

Dates
____

	BREAKFAST	LUNCH	DINNER	SNACKS
MON				
TUE				
WED				
THU				
FRI				
SAT				
SUN				

Shopping list

Note

Glycemic load
Diet planner

	BREAKFAST	LUNCH	DINNER	SNACKS
MON				
TUE				
WED				
THU				
FRI				
SAT				
SUN				

Shopping list

Note